SPRING IS HERE

LOIS LENSKI

Random House New York

Spring is here today!
Winter's gone away.

Spring is here today!
Open the door,
Come out and play —
Spring has come to stay!

Laughing, playing, dancing,
See the children gay —
Hear them singing,
"Spring is here,
Spring is here,
Spring is here today."

The sun is shining bright,
The apple tree has blossoms white,
Spring is here today.

The little birds are singing
Up in the leafy tree;
"Tweet, tweet, tweet," they sing
Just for you and me.

The warm south wind is blowing,
Sister's hair is flowing,
Brother's hat is going—
Spring is here today.

The milkman's horse goes prancing—
Spring is in the air!

Mother's clothes go dancing—
Spring is everywhere!

Pretty Robin Redbreast
Laid eggs in her nest.
Now there are
Baby birdies three,
Hungry as can be,
For me to see.

Up so high,
In the sky
Sister's swing goes up so high!
Oh my!

In the sky,
Up so high—
Brother's kite sails in the sky!
Oh my!

The baby calf goes tripping—
Spring is in the air!

Little lambs go skipping—
Spring is everywhere!

Pretty flowers blooming gay,
Sister picks a big bouquet!

Rabbits hopping,
Long ears flopping—
Spring is here today.

Easter bunny,
Very funny,
Pretty eggs will bring
On Easter in the spring.

Spade and rake
We will take
To the garden big.
With rake and spade
We will dig,
    dig,
        dig!

First we dig a row
Then in the seeds will go.
Dig, dig, dig,
Make a garden big!

The rain will rain,
The sun will shine,
Where we dig, dig, dig!
If we hoe,
Plants will grow
Big,
big,
BIG!

Over and under—
That's the way
To jump the rope
On a bright spring day.

Rolling round,
Rolling round,
See Brother's hoop
Roll round
On the ground!

Hop on one foot,
Hippety, hop!
Let's play hop-scotch
And never stop!

Throw and catch,
Throw and catch,
Catch and throw the ball.
Throw and catch,
Do not let it fall!

All the children
Are happy and gay!
Spring is here—
Spring has come to stay!